LEGO® DC COMICS SUPER HEROES

SIDEKICK SHOWDOWN!

BY TREY KING   ILLUSTRATED BY SEAN WANG

SCHOLASTIC INC.

THEY'RE OUTNUMBERED AND ARE GOING TO NEED HELP. BATMAN CALLS SOME FRIENDS FOR BACKUP.

THE HEROES HAVE SAVED THE DAY ONCE AGAIN. BATMAN TAKES THE JOKER TO JAIL.

HARLEY HOPS ON HER MOTORCYCLE AND TAKES OFF. SHE'LL HAVE THE JOKER FREE IN NO TIME . . .

TWO MORE SIDEKICKS—BATGIRL AND SUPERGIRL—JOIN ROBIN TO RESCUE THEIR FRIENDS.

THEY GET TO ARKHAM ASYLUM BEFORE THE BAD GUYS.

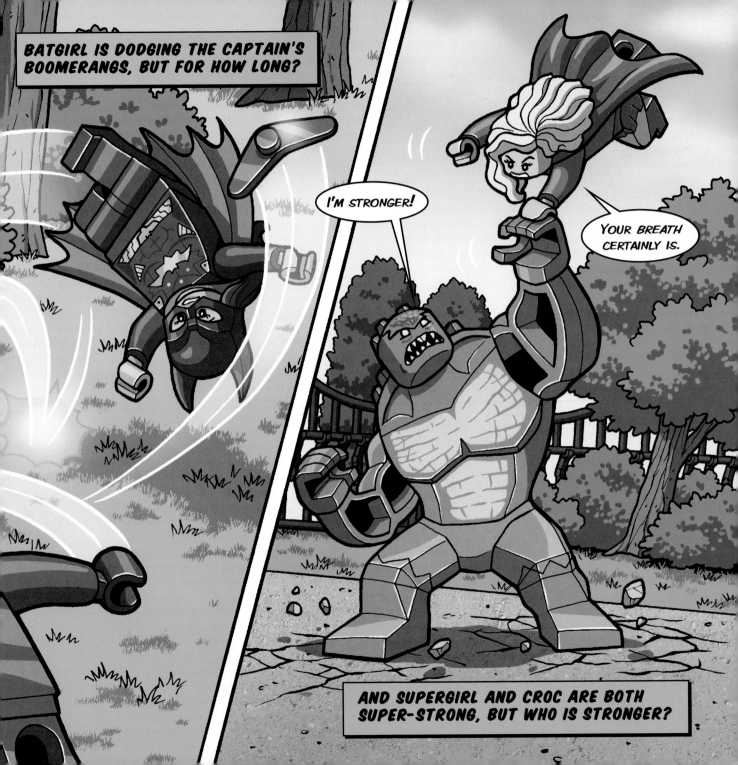

ELSEWHERE, THE SIDEKICKS SAVE THE HEROES. AFTER TELLING THEM EVERYTHING, SUPERMAN AND WONDER WOMAN ARE VERY THANKFUL.